Smithsonian LITTLE EXPLORER

Benjamin Franklin

The Man Behind the Lightning Rod

by Nancy Dickmann

PEBBLE
a capstone imprint

Little Explorer is published by Pebble, an imprint of Capstone.
1710 Roe Crest Drive,
North Mankato, Minnesota 56003
www.capstonepub.com

Library of Congress Cataloging-in-Publication data is available on the Library of Congress website.
ISBN 978-1-9771-1410-5 (library binding)
ISBN 978-1-9771-1785-4 (paperback)
ISBN 978-1-9771-1414-3 (eBook PDF)
Summary: Gives facts about Benjamin Franklin, his life as an inventor and Founding Father, and how his lightning rod invention led to new discoveries in electricity.

Image Credits
Alamy: Art Collection 3, 8, Science History Images, 13, 17, The Picture Art Collection, 10, The Protected Art Archive, 20; Bridgeman Images: © Look and Learn/Private Collection/Benjamin Franklin, Jackson, Peter (1922-2003), 18; Getty Images: Bettmann, 24, Tribune News Service/ Allentown Morning Call/Denise Sanchez, 7 (top); Granger: 15, 21, 22, Sarin Images, 11; iStockphoto: benoitb, 19, duncan1890, 9 (bottom); Library of Congress: 9 (top), 14, 26, 27; North Wind Picture Archives: 6, 7 (bottom), 12, 23; Shutterstock: Everett Historical, 5, Georgios Kollidas, cover (left), Lee Sneider Photo Images, 28, Marut Sayannikroth, cover (bottom right), Reeva, 4, Vectorpocket, cover (top right), YamabikaY, 29 (bottom); The New York Public Library: 25, 29 (top)

Design Elements by Shutterstock

Editorial Credits
Editor: Michelle Parkin; Designer: Sarah Bennett; Media Researcher: Svetlana Zhurkin; Production Specialist: Tori Abraham

Our very special thanks to Emma Grahn, Spark!Lab Manager, Lemelson Center for the Study of Invention and Innovation, National Museum of American History. Capstone would also like to thank Kealy Gordon, Product Development Manager, and the following at Smithsonian Enterprises: Ellen Nanney, Licensing Manager; Brigid Ferraro, Vice President, Education and Consumer Products; and Carol LeBlanc, Senior Vice President, Education and Consumer Products.

Printed in the United States of America.
PA99

TABLE OF CONTENTS

Bold words are in the glossary.

A SHOCKING INVENTION

Thunderstorms can be exciting. Thunder booms and lightning flashes across the sky. Lightning is a form of electricity. Lightning often strikes tall buildings.

Lightning strikes during a storm in Sydney, Australia.

Benjamin Franklin found a way to protect buildings from lightning. Franklin was many things. He was a **Founding Father** who helped shape our country. He was an author, a scientist, and a politician. He was also an **inventor**. Inventors are people who think up and create something new.

Benjamin Franklin in his study

EARLY LIFE

Benjamin with his parents and some of his siblings

Benjamin Franklin was born on January 17, 1706. He was one of 17 children. His family was not rich. Benjamin's father was a soap and candle maker. Benjamin stopped going to school when he was 10 years old. He worked with his father in his shop. But Benjamin still loved to read, write, and learn.

Benjamin was curious about how things worked. When he was 11, he invented swimming fins. Benjamin wore these wooden paddles on his hands to help him swim faster.

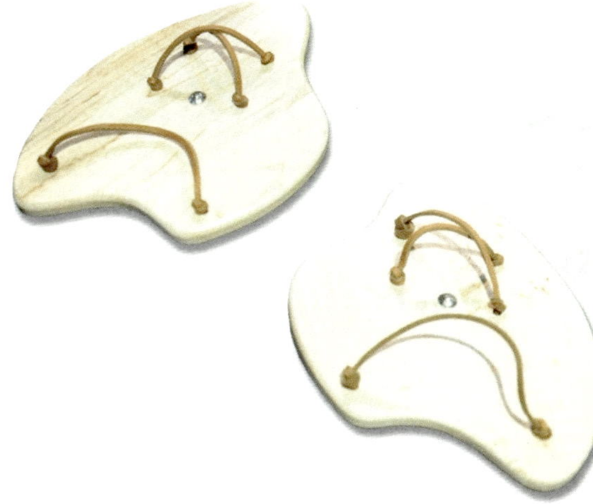

THE AMERICAN COLONIES

Benjamin's family lived in Boston. During this time, Boston was part of the Massachusetts Bay **colony**. There were 13 American colonies. They were ruled by Great Britain. After fighting for their independence, these colonies became the United States.

Boston was the biggest city in the American colonies.

BECOMING A PRINTER

Benjamin's older brother, James, ran a print shop. When Benjamin was 12, he became James's **apprentice**. Benjamin learned about printing. When he was 16, Benjamin wrote articles for James's newspaper. But James wouldn't print them. So Benjamin wrote them under a fake name—Mrs. Silence Dogood.

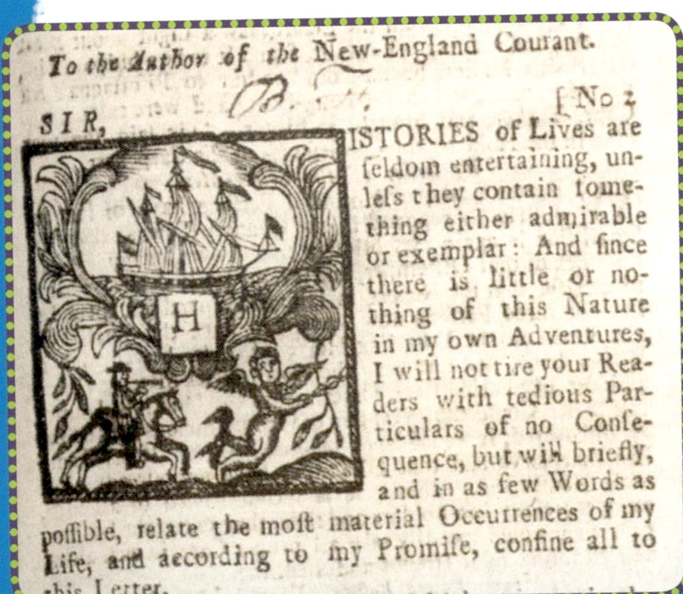

To the Author of the New-England Courant.

No 2.

SIR,

HISTORIES of Lives are ſeldom entertaining, unleſs they contain ſomething either admirable or exemplar: And ſince there is little or nothing of this Nature in my own Adventures, I will not tire your Readers with tedious Particulars of no Conſequence, but will briefly, and in as few Words as poſſible, relate the moſt material Occurrences of my Life, and according to my Promiſe, confine all to this Letter.

A letter by Mrs. Silence Dogood

Benjamin wrote 14 letters as Mrs. Silence Dogood in his brother's newspaper.

Franklin in his print shop

When Benjamin was 17, he moved to Philadelphia. He had many different jobs over the next few years, including working as a bookkeeper and shopkeeper. In 1732, Benjamin started his own print shop. He printed *Poor Richard's Almanack*. It included puzzles, weather reports, and witty sayings.

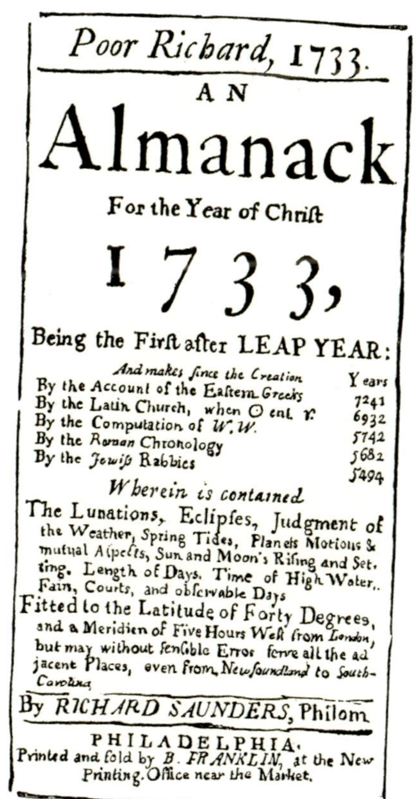

Poor Richard, 1733.

AN

Almanack

For the Year of Christ

1733,

Being the First after LEAP YEAR:

And makes since the Creation Years

By the Account of the Eastern Greeks 7241

By the Latin Church, when ☉ ent. ♈ 6932

By the Computation of W. W. 5742

By the Roman Chronology 5682

By the Jewish Rabbies 5494

Wherein is contained

The Lunations, Eclipses, Judgment of the Weather, Spring Tides, Planets Motions & mutual Aspects, Sun and Moon's Rising and Setting, Length of Days, Time of High Water, Fairs, Courts, and observable Days

Fitted to the Latitude of Forty Degrees, and a Meridien of Five Hours West from *London*, but may without sensible Error serve all the adjacent Places, even from *Newfoundland* to *South-Carolina*.

By *RICHARD SAUNDERS*, Philom.

PHILADELPHIA.

Printed and sold by *B. FRANKLIN*, at the New Printing-Office near the Market.

Benjamin published *Poor Richard's Almanack* for 25 years.

THE FRANKLIN STOVE

In his spare time, Franklin liked to invent things. He had many new ideas. Around 1742 Franklin invented a new kind of stove.

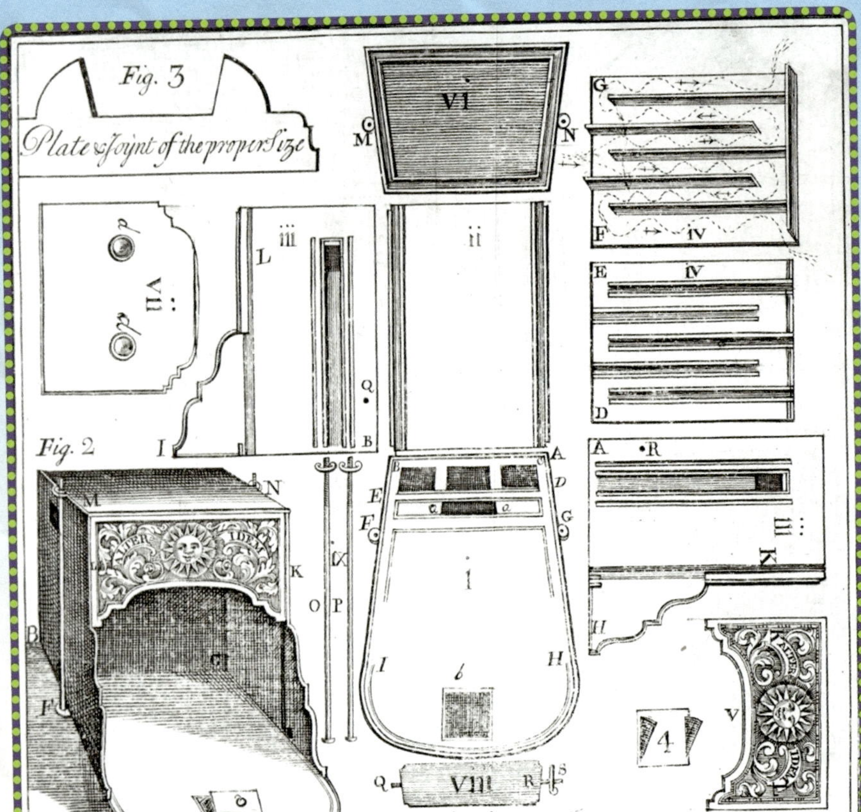

Franklin drew the parts he used to make the Franklin stove.

A man warming himself in front of a Franklin stove

During this time, people used fireplaces to heat their homes. The Franklin stove was placed in the middle of the living room or inside the fireplace. It didn't need as much wood as other fireplaces. Franklin's invention gave out more heat with less smoke. Soon, many people used Franklin stoves in their homes.

ELECTRICITY

In 1746 Franklin started to study electricity. At that time, not much was known about electricity. People knew that they could make sparks by rubbing certain materials together. But they didn't know how to control electricity. They didn't understand how to use it. Franklin wanted to find the answers.

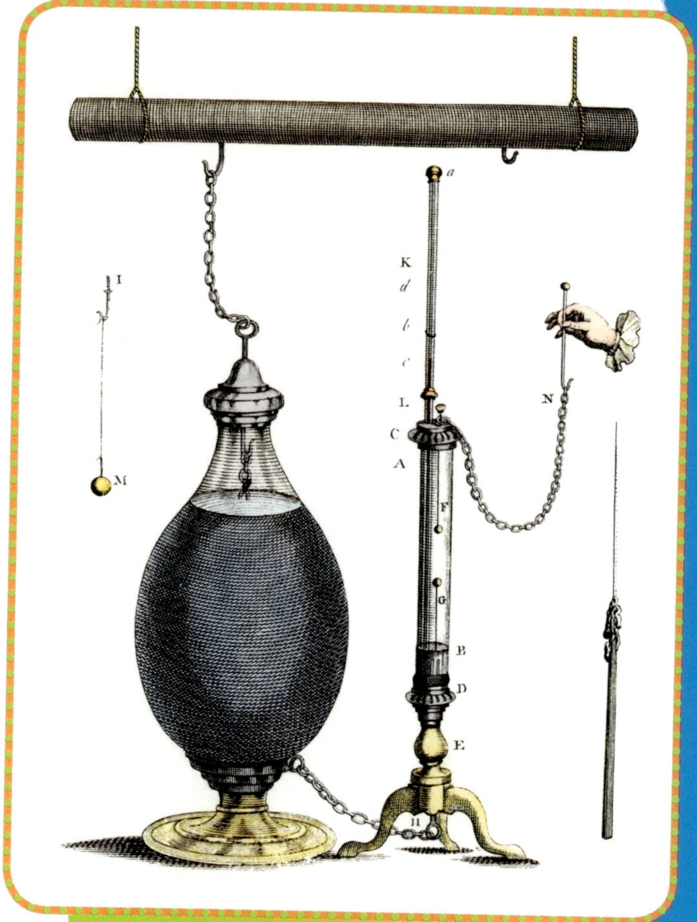

One of Franklin's electrical experiments

Franklin studied electricity in the mid-1700s.

Franklin retired from his printing business in 1749. He was 42 years old. Franklin wanted to focus on science, experiments, and inventions full time.

CONTROLLING LIGHTNING

Scientists were working on ways to control electricity. Franklin thought a lot about lightning. He believed it was a form of electricity. If it was, maybe it could be controlled too.

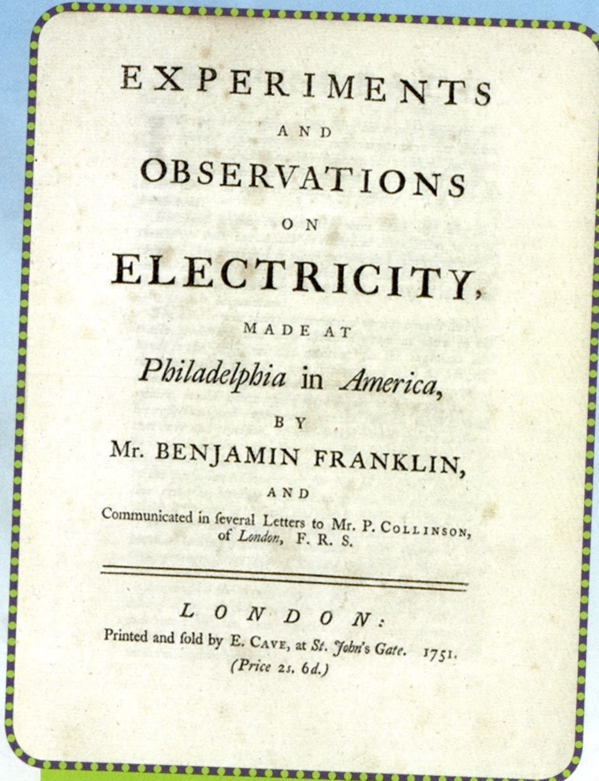

EXPERIMENTS
AND
OBSERVATIONS
ON
ELECTRICITY,
MADE AT
Philadelphia in *America*,
BY
Mr. BENJAMIN FRANKLIN,
AND
Communicated in ſeveral Letters to Mr. P. COLLINSON, of *London*, F. R. S.

LONDON:
Printed and ſold by E. CAVE, at *St. John's Gate*. 1751.
(Price 2s. 6d.)

Franklin's work on lightning and electricity can be found in *Experiments and Observations on Electricity.*

Lightning can be dangerous. During Franklin's time, lightning strikes caused many fires. They destroyed buildings and trees. Franklin wanted to protect people. He had an idea. Franklin wanted to put a metal rod on a building's roof. He believed that lightning would strike the rod. The electricity would travel safely into the ground. It wouldn't damage the building.

When lightning struck the rod, electricity traveled through a wire and down to the ground.

THE KITE EXPERIMENT

Franklin's lightning rod was a good idea. But he had to test it. He wanted to use the top of a tall church. There was only one problem—it was still being built. Franklin didn't want to wait. He decided to use a kite instead.

In June 1752, Franklin tied a metal key to a kite. The key would **attract** the lightning. To protect himself, Franklin held onto a silk ribbon. It was tied to the kite's string. Silk does not **conduct** electricity. Then he took his kite out into a thunderstorm.

Franklin came up with the words *conductor*, *charge*, and *electrify*.

Franklin used a kite and a metal key to find out if lightning was a form of electricity.

LIGHTNING RODS

Franklin's kite was not struck by lightning. The kite's string got wet in the rain. The metal key picked up the electricity in the air. When Franklin put his hand near the key, he felt a spark. This proved that lightning was a form of electricity. Franklin's experiment was a success.

Franklin shared his findings. Soon, buildings in Boston put up lightning rods. The idea spread through the American colonies.

Franklin put a lightning rod on a home's roof.

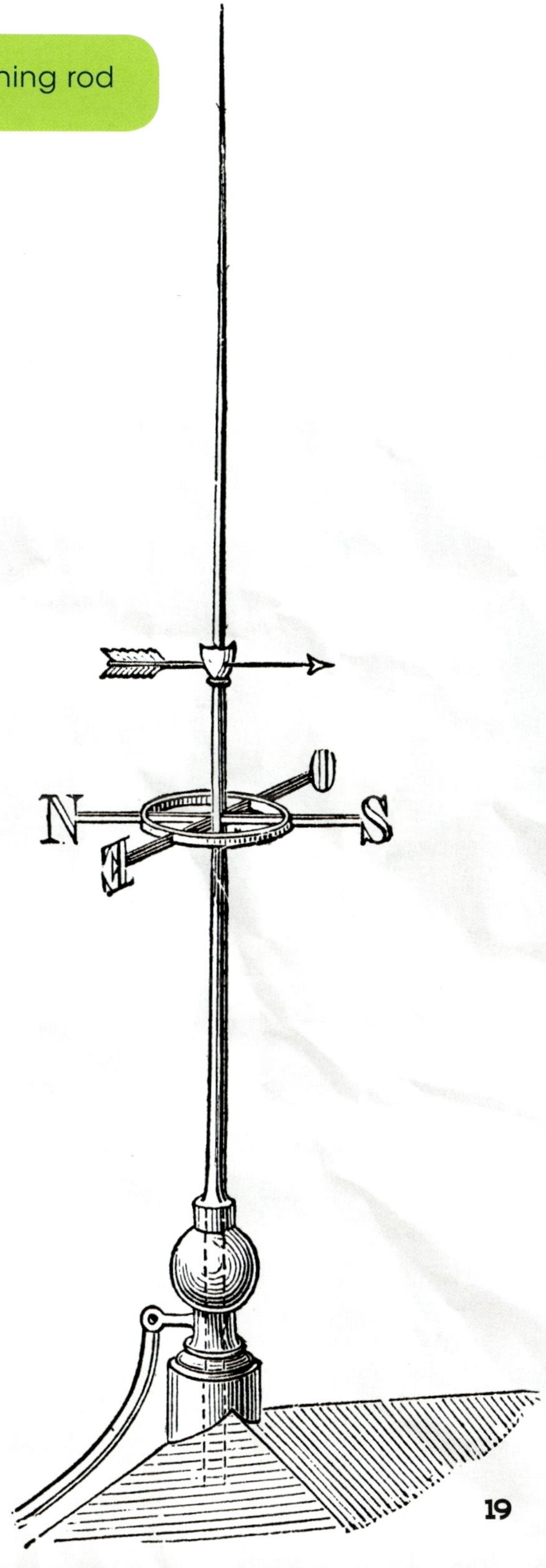

Pointed lightning rod

POINTED OR BLUNT LIGHTNING RODS

Franklin thought lightning rods with sharp points worked best. British scientists disagreed. The British king had a **blunt** lightning rod put on his palace. Soon, lightning rods meant more than just protecting homes from lightning. People who supported the British king used blunt lightning rods. People against British rule had pointed lightning rods on their homes and businesses.

OTHER INVENTIONS

Franklin was full of ideas. He invented an **odometer**. He used it to measure the distance between postal stations. Franklin's odometer was attached to the wheel of a horse-drawn carriage. Its measurements helped make more accurate maps.

Franklin played the glass armonica.

Wine glasses filled with water can make music. A person rubs the rim of the glass with a finger to make sounds. Franklin invented the glass armonica. Using this instrument, a person could play many glasses at once.

Ludwig van Beethoven and Wolfgang Mozart wrote music for the glass armonica.

"Of all my inventions, the glass armonica has given me the greatest personal satisfaction."

—Benjamin Franklin

FOUNDING FATHER

The American colonies were controlled by Great Britain. Many colonists wanted to be free from British rule. They wanted to form their own country. Great Britain did not agree. This led to the **Revolutionary War** (1775–1783).

Franklin helped the colonists in many ways. Franklin became a politician. He was one of America's Founding Fathers. He helped write the **Declaration of Independence**. He designed our country's first penny.

Franklin's penny showed a chain of 13 links. It stood for the 13 original states.

Franklin traveled to France during the Revolutionary War. He helped convince the French king to help the colonies.

BIFOCALS AND MORE

Politics kept Franklin busy. But he never stopped inventing. In 1783 Franklin invented a new type of eyeglasses. They were called bifocals. Each lens was divided into two parts. The upper half helped the wearer see far away. The lower half was for seeing up close. Bifocals are still used today.

Franklin made notes and drawings of his inventions.

Franklin wanted to invent things that made life easier. His house had tall bookshelves. Franklin invented a long wooden arm. The arm could grab books from the highest shelves.

SOME OF FRANKLIN'S INVENTIONS

1717
swimming fins

around 1742
the Franklin stove

around 1749
the lightning rod

1760s
an odometer

1762
the glass armonica

1783
bifocals

1785
long wooden arm to grab books

LATER YEARS

Franklin spent almost 10 years in France. He returned to Philadelphia in 1785. By this time, Franklin was famous. People admired his work on electricity. They respected his work in politics. They liked his inventions.

Franklin returned to Philadelphia after living in France.

In 1787 Franklin represented the state of Pennsylvania and helped write the U.S. **Constitution**. In his later years, Franklin kept reading, thinking, and writing. Benjamin Franklin died on April 17, 1790. He was 84 years old.

Franklin helped write the U.S. Constitution in 1787.

"Do not fear mistakes. You will know failure. Continue to reach out."

—Benjamin Franklin

FRANKLIN'S LEGACY

Franklin was a rich man. After he died, he left money to cities for scholarships and other projects.

We owe a lot to Benjamin Franklin. He helped found our country. His discoveries inspired scientists for generations. And his many inventions made our lives better.

A statue of Benjamin Franklin in Philadelphia

Benjamin Franklin in 1783

Benjamin Franklin's face is on the $100 bill.

GLOSSARY

apprentice (uh-PREN-tiss)—someone who learns a trade by working with a skilled person

attract (uh-TRAKT)—to pull something toward something else

blunt (BLUHNT)—not sharp

colony (KAH-luh-nee)—the 13 territories where people lived in North America before the Revolutionary War; the colonies were ruled by Great Britain

conduct (kuhn-DUHKT)—when electricity easily travels through a material

Constitution (kon-stuh-TOO-shuhn)—the written system of laws that states the rights of people and powers of government

Declaration of Independence (dek-luh-RAY-shuhn OHV in-di-PEN-duhnss)—a document that declares the United States a free and independent country

Founding Father (FOUN-ding FAH-thuhr)—one of a handful of men who were important in helping the colonies become one country

inventor (in-VENT-ohr)—someone who thinks up and creates something new

odometer (oh-DAH-muh-tur)—a tool that shows how far something has traveled

Revolutionary War (rev-uh-LOO-shuhn-air-ee WOHR)—the American colonies' fight for freedom against Great Britain; the Revolutionary War lasted from 1775 to 1783

CRITICAL THINKING QUESTIONS

1. Franklin wrote letters to his brother's newspaper under a different name. What was it? Why did Franklin change his name?

2. During Franklin's time, why would someone want a pointed lightning rod on a home or business?

3. Benjamin Franklin liked to invent things that made life easier. Think of a new invention that would make your life easier. What would it do?

READ MORE

Jensen, Belinda. *A Party for Clouds: Thunderstorms.* Minneapolis: Millbrook Press, 2016.

Murray, Laura K. *The Declaration of Independence.* North Mankato, MN: Capstone, 2020.

Rosen, Michael J. *A Ben of All Trades: The Most Inventive Boyhood of Benjamin Franklin.* Somerville, MA: Candlewick, 2020.

INTERNET SITES

All About Benjamin Franklin
https://kidzfeed.com/benjamin-franklin-facts-for-kids/

Benjamin Franklin
https://www.dkfindout.com/us/science/famous-scientists/benjamin-franklin/

INDEX